I Am Porkchop

visit us at www.flyingrhino.com

Copyright © Flying Rhinoceros, Inc.

All rights reserved. Farmer Bob and Flying Rhinoceros are trademarks of Flying Rhinoceros, Inc.

Mailing Address: P.O. Box 3989
Portland, Oregon, U.S.A.
97208-3989

E-mail Address: bigfan@flyingrhino.com

Library of Congress Control Number:
98-094849

ISBN 1-883772-17-6
ISBN 1-883772-79-6 Farmer Bob On The Farm series

Printed in Mexico

I am Porkchop Brown.

3

I play music with my band.

Tiny plays the bass.

Link plays the fiddle.

Boom Boom plays the drums.

We play music in the morning.

We play music at noon.

13

We play music at night.

Farmer Bob and the animals love music.
They love to sing with us.

17

The pigs sing oink, oink, oink.

The cows sing moo, moo, moo.

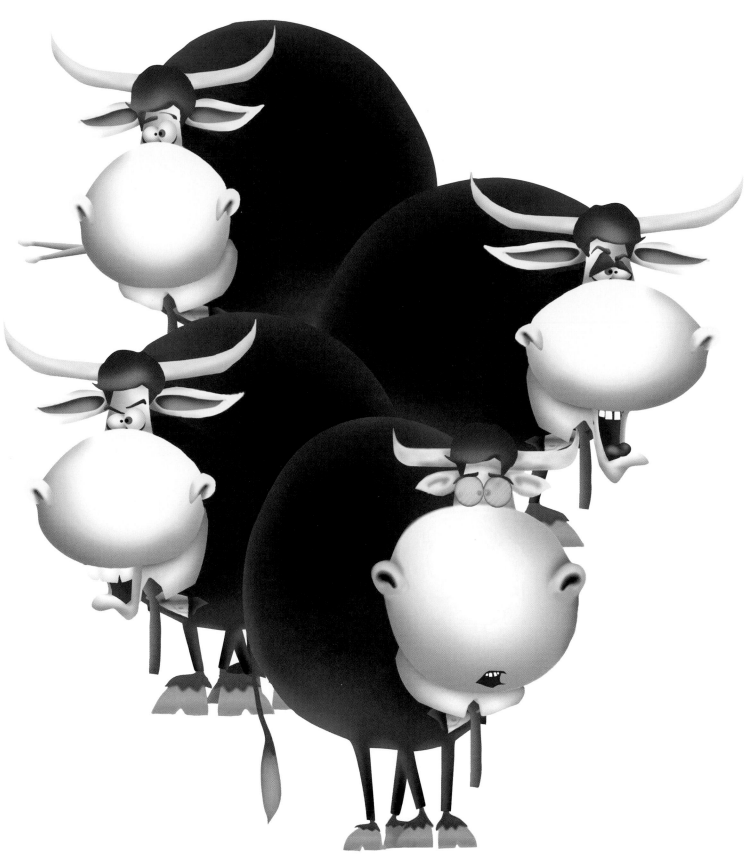

The ducks sing quack, quack, quack.

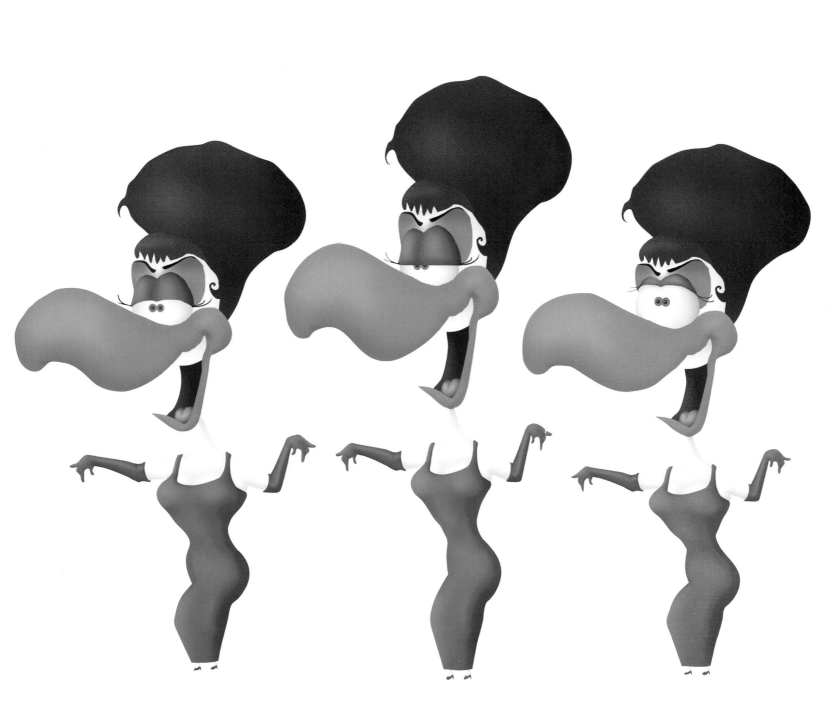

23

The rooster sings cock-a-doodle-doo.

The dog sings woof, woof, woof.

The cat sings meow, meow, meow.

The animals sing and dance all day long.

GLOSSARY

moo

meow

woof

oink

quack

cock-a-doodle-doo

ABOUT THE AUTHORS AND ARTISTS

Ben Adams says farm animals are smelly, but he likes to draw pictures of them anyway. Ben lives in his very own house in Portland, Oregon. He likes to spend time in his backyard pruning, watering, and sculpting his trees into giant farm animals. Someday, he hopes to have his own tree farm and change his name to Farmer Ben.

Julie Hansen grew up in Tillamook, Oregon, and knows a lot about cows. Although she has never actually owned a cow, she has raised almost everything else: dogs, cats, chickens, rabbits, frogs, rats, mice, fish, ducks, snakes, squirrels, and the occasional muskrat. She lives in Salem, Oregon with her husband, Mark, their son, Chance, two cats, and a dog the size of a cat.

Kyle Holveck lives in Newberg, Oregon, with his wife, Raydene, and their daughter, Kylie. In Newberg, there are lots of farms and animals. Kyle's favorite farm animal is the rhinoceros, which *we* know is not really a farm animal. Because his house is too small to keep a rhinoceros, Kyle has a chihuahua named Pedro instead.

Aaron Peeples's hero is Farmer Bob. He says that any man who can look good wearing overalls day after day is definitely a great man. Aaron is currently attending college in Portland, Oregon, and he enjoys drawing farm animals at Flying Rhinoceros between classes.

Ray Nelson thinks cows and pigs are really neat. He also thinks bacon and hamburgers are really neat. (We haven't told him where bacon and hamburgers come from yet.) Ray lives in Wilsonville, Oregon, with his wife, Theresa. They have two children, Alexandria and Zach, and a mutant dog named Molly.

CONTRIBUTORS: Melody Burchyski, Jennii Childs, Paul Diener, Lynnea "Mad Dog" Eagle, MaryBeth Habecker, Mark Hansen, Lee Lagle, Mari McBurney, Mike McLane, Chris Nelson, Hillery Nye, Kari Rasmussen, Steve Sund, and Ranjy Thomas

visit us online:
www.
flyingrhino.com
or call 1-800-537-4466